The Magic Spell

by David Lewman
illustrated by Sharon Ross
with Anastasios Gionis
and Carl A. Braxton

SCHOLASTIC INC.

New York Toronto London Auckland Sydney
Mexico City New Delhi Hong Kong Buenos Aires

CHAPTER 1

"Can you reach it, Philip?" whispered Lil. She was kneeling on the floor underneath the kitchen table in Tommy's house. Tommy was next to her, and Phil was balancing on their backs.

"Almost, Lillian," answered Phil. His arm stretched up to reach the top of the table.

Tommy grunted. "Could you please hurry, Phil? 'Cause, um, you're kinda heavy."

"Yeah," said Lil, "you weigh more than an ella-fat!"

"I do not," said Phil. "I weigh the same as you, Lillian!"

"No you don't, Philip!" said Lil.

"Do so!"

"Do NOT!"

A large bowlful of pumpkin pulp sat on the table. Didi had scooped the pulp out and plopped it into the bowl. She hummed as she happily carved a friendly face into the pumpkin.

"You call that scary, Deed?" Betty said with a snort. "Tomorrow's Halloween, not Valentine's Day." Betty was carving her pumpkin to look like a vampire.

Didi finished cutting a wide, smiling mouth. "I don't want it to frighten the babies," she said. "You know what Dr. Lipschitz says. . . ."

"'I'm full of hot air'?" suggested Betty.

Didi sighed. "According to *The Lipschitz Guide to Holiday Trauma*," she said, "on Halloween, big fears can grow from little deeds, just as mighty pumpkins sprout from tiny pumpkin seeds. . . ."

Didi and Betty didn't notice Phil's

small hand creeping onto the table top. He reached into the bowl of pulp, grabbed a handful of the slimy stuff, and pulled it beneath the table.

Phil popped the pulp into his mouth. "Mmm," he said as orange goo dripped down his chin. "Even better than worms!"

"My turn, Philip," said Lil.

"Hold your diapies, Lillian," answered Phil, reaching up for more. But just as his hand reached the bowl, Lil abruptly rolled out from under him.

"Take that, Philip!" she said. Phil grabbed at the bowl as he fell, flipping it and spilling pumpkin pulp everywhere.

"Squishy stuff for everybody!" cried Tommy, giggling. The three babies picked up the pulp and began stuffing handfuls into their mouths.

Didi peeked under the tablecloth. "Look at this! What a mess!" she said.

"We'd better get this cleaned up."

"Okay, boys and ghouls," said Betty, picking up the twins. "Back to the playpen you go!" Didi picked up Tommy and followed Betty.

The living room was decorated for Halloween. Fake bats hung from the ceiling. A picture of a witch riding on a broomstick was taped to the wall, and the curtains were draped with fake spiderwebs.

"BOO!" Stu yelled as he jumped out from behind the curtain. He was wearing a mask with a long, pointy nose. Everyone laughed.

Stu sighed, disappointed. "I scared you, right, buddy?" he asked Tommy. But Tommy just giggled and pulled on the nose of Stu's mask. "Hmm," Stu said, "maybe if I just glue a bigger wart on the nose. . . . I'll be in the basement."

Didi rolled her eyes. "Stu's been like

this all week," she said. "He's more excited about Halloween than the kids are!" Betty and Didi put the babies in the playpen.

On the couch Stu's brother, Drew, was reading a newspaper. His wife, Charlotte, sat next to him, talking on her cell phone.

"You two party poopers are missing all the pumpkin carving!" said Betty as she and Didi returned to the kitchen.

"We'll be there in a second," Charlotte said, going right back to her phone conversation.

Dressed in a princess costume with a cape and a jeweled crown, Angelica tiptoed over to a bowl of Halloween candy. She checked to make sure her parents weren't paying attention, and then she stuck her hand into the bowl.

"*Princess . . . ,*" said Drew.

"Yes, Daddy?" said Angelica, quickly

snatching a handful of candy and hiding it behind her back.

"I already told you," said Drew. "Halloween is *tomorrow*. Put the candy back."

"Can't I have just one teeny, tiny piece?" Angelica pleaded. "Please, please, please, best Daddy?"

Drew smiled. "Well, all right. But just one."

"You're the bestest daddy in the whole wild world!" said Angelica as she dug through the bowl for the most delicious-looking piece of candy. She took a bite, chewed, and then spit it out.

"Blech! Yucky coconut!" she said, sticking out her tongue.

In the playpen Tommy and the twins were playing with rubber spiders. Chuckie was bouncing his bouncy ball. Dil was drooling on a pumpkin-shaped squeak toy.

"Yucky, yucky!" Dil blabbered happily.

"Why does your house look so funny, Tommy?" asked Lil.

"Yeah," said Phil, "and why is your dad acting so silly?"

"I don't know," said Tommy.

Angelica sauntered over to the playpen, still holding the chewed-up piece of coconut candy. "You dumb babies don't know nothin'!" she said. "It's Hallomean!"

"Hallomean?" asked Tommy. "What's that?"

Angelica sighed. "Hallomean is when you get dressed up and go tricka-treating and get lots and lotsa candy!"

"CANDY?!" the babies cried at once. "We loooove candy!"

"Speaking of candy," said Phil, "you gonna eat that?" Before Angelica could answer, he snatched the coconut candy from her hand and popped it into his mouth.

"Yucky!" said Dil.

"Nope, yummy," said Phil.

Just then the doorbell rang. "I'll get it!" yelled Angelica.

Stu came running up from the basement. "Wait! Wait! Me first!" Stu positioned Betty's vampire jack-o'-lantern in front of his face. "Okay, open the door on three, Angelica. One . . . two . . ."

CHAPTER 2

Chas Finster was just about to press the doorbell a second time when the front door suddenly flew open.

"BOO!"

"AHH!" Chas and Chuckie screamed. Standing in the doorway was a horrible monster with a pumpkin head! Its mouth was wide open, showing its long, sharp teeth.

"Happy Halloween!" said Stu, lowering the pumpkin he'd been holding in front of his face. But he was still wearing his monster mask underneath.

"AHH!" Chas and Chuckie screamed again.

Stu took the mask off, and Chas

sighed in relief. "See, Chuckie?" he said. "It's just Tommy's dad. He was playing a Halloween joke on us. Not a very funny joke, but a joke."

Chuckie still looked scared. Chas carried him inside, where he stared wide-eyed at the Halloween decorations—bats, witches, ghosts, spiders—all kinds of creepy stuff. Chuckie ran over to Tommy, Phil, and Lil.

Kimi let go of Kira's hand and followed Chuckie. "Look at all the neat stuff!" she said. Chuckie shuddered.

Betty came out from the kitchen looking for the pumpkin she'd been carving. "Stu, I'm not done with that yet," she said, taking the jack-o'-lantern. "I want to add a few more fangs."

Chas watched as Chuckie backed away from a hanging bat decoration. "I'm afraid Halloween might be too scary for Chuckie," he said. "I don't know if taking him to the amusement park tomorrow night is such a good idea."

Betty chuckled. "I always say the best way to keep from being scared is to be even *more* scary than what you're scared of."

"What do you mean?" asked Kira.

"Let's dress these pups up as monsters for Halloween. That way, they'll think they're more scary than anything they see."

"That's a great idea!" Kira said. "Kimi could be a witch, and Chuckie can be a . . . werewolf."

Chas looked worried. "A werewolf?" he asked. "I don't know."

While the grown-ups were talking, Angelica tiptoed over to the candy bowl and tried to sneak another piece of candy, but her mother saw her.

"Angelica!" yelled Charlotte. "We told you no more candy! If we catch you again, no trick-or-treating tomorrow. Understand?"

"Yes, Mommy, dearest," said Angelica, smiling as sweetly as she could. Then she stomped over to the babies, grumbling to herself.

Chuckie noticed Angelica's pink sparkly costume. "Angelica," he said, "how come you're dressed like that?"

Angelica rolled her eyes. "How many times do I have to eggsplain Hallomean to you diaper brains? You have to dress up so you can get candy! I'm a princess 'cause princesses get the most candy."

"Do we all get to be princesses?" asked Chuckie hopefully.

"Nope," answered Angelica. "Only me. You, 'Fraidy-Cat Finster, are going to be a werewuff."

"A werewuff?" asked Chuckie. "What's a werewuff?"

"Oh," answered Angelica, "just a mean, scary monster that gots a hairy face and pointy ears and howls at the full moon and steals babies and gets hunted down in the forest by growed-ups!"

Chuckie's eyes got as big as saucers. Being a werewuff didn't sound like such a good idea to him.

"Now," Angelica said, "do you babies wanna know the bestest part about

dressing up for Hallomean?"

Everyone except Chuckie nodded eagerly. Angelica looked around as though she was going to tell them a big secret. Then she motioned for them to come closer.

"Whatever you dress up as," Angelica said quietly, "you turn into for *real!*"

Chuckie looked terrified. "You mean? . . ."

Angelica nodded. "That's right, Finster. Tomorrow you're gonna turn into a werewuff forever and ever! And EVER!"

CHAPTER 3

That night Chuckie lay in his bed, tossing and turning. A full moon was shining outside his window.

"I don't want to turn into a were-wuff. . . . I don't want to turn into a werewuff," he muttered to himself. Slowly he fell asleep. . . .

Chuckie's hands felt itchy. When he scratched them, he saw that they were covered in long brown hair! Horrified, he watched as his fingers curled into claws. His ears wiggled, and when he touched them, they felt pointy. Chuckie climbed onto his dresser and peered into the mirror. His whole body was covered with fur! He was as furry as his dog, Fifi, only

Chuckie's fur was dark and straight instead of white and curly.

Chuckie sniffed the air with his snout and looked out the window at the big, bright moon. The moon was tugging at him, beckoning him to come outside. Chuckie put on his glasses, opened his window, and slid down the drainpipe to the ground below.

Looking up at the moon, Chuckie let out a long howl. Then he loped off across the yard.

In their bedroom Phil and Lil were sleeping soundly, wearing matching pajamas. Something scratched at their window.

"Stop scratchin', Philip," mumbled Lil.

"I'm not, Lillian," grumbled Phil.

It was Chuckie-the-Werewuff! He pried open the window, climbed in, and crept toward the twins.

Suddenly they both sat up in bed.

"Chuckie, what are you doing?" Lil asked.

"Well, Phil and Lil, as you can see, I'm a werewuff now, so, um . . . I gots to steal you and take you to the forest," said Chuckie. He let out a weak howl.

Phil and Lil looked at each other. "We're not going to let you steal us!" cried Lil.

Phil agreed. "Yeah! Let's get him, Lil!"

Chuckie gasped and jumped through the window. He lowered himself to the ground on a vine of ivy and ran down the path. Phil and Lil chased after him.

Chuckie-the-Werewuff ran toward a deep, dark forest. Maybe now that I'm a werewuff, he thought, I won't be a-scared of the dark. He looked up at the thick, black branches swaying overhead. Nope, he thought, still scary.

When he looked behind him, he saw Phil and Lil still chasing after him.

Behind them more people were following—Angelica, Tommy, Susie, Kimi—even Reptar! Tommy was shining his clown flashlight in Chuckie's direction. Oh, no, Chuckie thought, not the scary clown flashlight! He heard them yelling, "Get him! Get the werewuff!"

Chuckie tried to climb a tree, but he slid back down the trunk. The mob surrounded him. Just then Chuckie's dad stepped forward, holding a huge jack-o'-lantern.

"Whew," Chuckie sighed. My daddy will protect me, he thought.

"Sorry, Chuckie," Chas said. "But I have to keep you from hurting anyone. Now, get inside this pumpkin. . . ." Chas took off the pumpkin lid and stepped toward Chuckie.

"No! No!" cried Chuckie. . . .

"NO!" yelled Chuckie, waking himself up. It was morning, and he was tangled

up in his sheets. He looked at his hands—
no fur! He patted his ears—no points! He
touched his nose—no snout! "Whew! It
was only a nightscare," he told himself,
relieved.

Suddenly Chuckie heard a loud cackling sound right outside his door. Slowly

the door creaked open, and Kimi crept in. Her face was painted green and she was wearing a long, black dress and a tall, black, pointed hat.

"Happy Hallomean, Chuckie!" she shouted, and then she cackled again.

Chuckie peeked out from under his covers. "Kimi?" he asked. "Is that you?"

"There is no more Kimi!" she said in a raspy voice. "There is only Kimi-Witch!"

"Oh, no!" Chuckie cried. "Angelica was right!"

Chas came into the room carrying a werewolf costume. He ruffled Chuckie's red hair. "There's my little werewolf!"

Chuckie pulled the covers over his head.

CHAPTER 4

Tommy loved his shiny black cape. He and his dad were dressed up as vampires for Halloween.

"Okay, let's see you use that cape," said Stu. He showed Tommy how to grab the edge of the cape and pull it up to hide the bottom half of his face.

"That's my little vampire!" said Stu, holding his big cape up the same way. "One, two, three . . . switch!"

Stu and Tommy dropped their capes and pulled them up to their eyes the opposite way. "And switch!"

"Stu, it's time to go to the amusement park!" Didi called from the kitchen.

Stu picked up Tommy and set him

down with the other babies. "Be right back, Count Tomcula," he said in a deep voice. "I've got to adjust my fangs." He opened his mouth to show his teeth. "I vant to suck your blood!" Tommy giggled.

"Stu, are you scaring the babies?" Didi called.

"No, Deed," said Stu as he went into the kitchen.

"Wow, you guys," said Tommy, "being a monster is even better than being a baby! Babies don't gots a neat vampy-ire cape!"

Phil and Lil, dressed in black bat costumes, flapped their wings. Dil wriggled around on the floor, dressed as a black spider. Kimi cackled her witch's cackle. Chuckie, dressed as a werewolf, looked miserable.

"Yeah, well, I don't gots a neat cape," said Chuckie. "All I gots is a bunch of fur, and it's hot and itchy under here."

Tommy toddled over to his friend, swooshing his cape back and forth as he walked. "Cheer up, Chuckiewuff," he said. "I bet werewuffs get to do lotsa fun stuff."

"Oh yeah, like what?" asked Chuckie, scratching at his costume.

"Well . . . ," Tommy said, "I don't know yet, but I bet we'll find out soon."

"At least your daddy's a vampy-ire like you," said Chuckie. "I don't know what my daddy is, but he's not a werewuff."

Chas was struggling with a stroller by the front door. He was dressed as a Japanese samurai warrior in a long red robe with wide shoulders and a sash tied around the waist. He kept getting his arms tangled up in the big sleeves. Fifi was next to him, dressed as a ghost-dog.

Chuckie frowned. "Even Fifi is gonna

turn into something I don't want her to be. How will I be able to see her if she turns into a ghost?"

While Angelica's parents helped pack up the strollers, she crept toward the bowl of candy on the table.

"Angelica!" yelled Drew and Charlotte at the same time.

Charlotte walked over to her daughter, looking stern. "That's it," she said. "We warned you. No trick-or-treating at the amusement park."

Drew looked as though he wanted to give Angelica one more chance, but Charlotte glared at him. "Your mother's right," he said weakly. "You disobeyed, so no trick-or-treating."

Angelica tried looking really, really sad. She squeezed her eyes tight, trying to force a tear to come out, but her parents went back to getting ready for the amusement park without noticing.

Angelica let out a loud sigh. "I'll get my grubby hands on the sweet stuff if it's the last thing I do!" she grumbled as she shuffled away.

"Angelica," said Chuckie, "I don't wanna be a werewuff. Can't I be myself again?"

"Stop whining, Finster!" growled Angelica. "What do I look like, some kind of magical princess?"

"Um . . . yes," said Chuckie. "You do."

Angelica caught a glimpse of the crystal candy bowl making rainbows on the walls. Hmm . . . I'm a magical princess, all right, she thought to herself. "You know what, Finster?" Angelica said. "Since I'm a princess, I can turn you back into a little crybaby—"

"That's great, Angelica!" said Tommy. "I guess being a princess made you nice."

"If—," Angelica continued.

"If what?" asked Chuckie nervously.

"*If* you babies gimme all your tricka-treat candy!"

The babies gasped.

"But we love Hallomean candy," said Lil. "Especially the gummy worms."

"I'll give you my candy, Angelica," said Chuckie.

But Angelica shook her head. "That's not good enough!" she said. "You *all* hafta gimme your candy, or else *nobody* gets to be a dumb baby ever again!"

CHAPTER 5

"Oh, look! There's an apple-bobbing contest!" said Stu, excited. The group had arrived at the Halloween-themed amusement park dressed in their costumes. Even Grandpa Lou and Lulu were dressed up—as Frankenstein's monster and his bride.

"Now, Stu," said Didi, "we came here to take the babies trick-or-treating, remember?"

Stu took Didi by the hand. "Come on, Deed," he pleaded. "This is my only chance to bob for apples while wearing fangs!" He smiled, pointing to the sharp plastic teeth in his mouth. "I'm sure to win! You've gotta come watch!"

"Go ahead," said Grandpa Lou. "We'll take the sprouts to see some of the sights and meet you back here in half an hour."

Stu eagerly led the other grown-ups off to the apple-bobbing, while the babies followed Lou and Lulu.

Chuckie stayed so close to Tommy that he kept tripping on Tommy's cape. "Aren't you a-scared?" he asked.

"Uh-uh," said Tommy, shaking his head. "Now that I'm a monster, I'm not a-scared of anything."

"Well, I'm a monster too," said Chuckie. "But I'm a-scared."

Tommy's neighbor Susie Carmichael let go of her dad's hand and ran to greet her friends. "Happy Halloween!" she said, fluttering her angel wings. "We're going to Trick-or-Treat Street. Wanna come?"

Angelica looked up at Grandpa Lou,

trying to make her eyes as big and cute as possible. "Can I, Grandpa? Pretty please?" she begged.

"Sorry, Angelica," he answered. "But your parents said that if you're good, maybe they'll take you later."

"Fine," said Angelica, crossing her arms. "I'll tell my daddy I was a little angel."

Lulu leaned down. "They asked us to give them a *full* report, sweetheart. A full report."

"Okay, okay," sighed Angelica. "I'll be good."

"Sure you will," said Susie, skipping off to Trick-or-Treat Street.

Grandpa Lou, Lulu, and the babies walked in the other direction, toward the kiddie haunted house. "What do you say, mini-monsters? Want to go inside?" asked Grandpa Lou.

Chuckie looked up at the entrance to the haunted house. There was a picture of a friendly, smiling ghost above the door. "No!" Chuckie shouted.

Grandpa Lou turned to Lulu. "Ain't that cute?" he said. "Little sprout still hasn't learned any new words. He says 'no' even when he means 'yes.'" The two grown-ups headed inside with the other babies.

Chuckie had no choice. Shivering, he followed them into the haunted house.

CHAPTER 6

"*Commmme iiiiiiiiin!*" moaned a park employee dressed as a ghost. Chuckie grabbed Angelica's arm.

"Leggo of me, Finster!" Angelica said. "You gots more a-portant things to worry about than this stupid little haunted house for babies. Like getting me candy!" She shook Chuckie off and ran ahead.

Silently the ghost pointed down a dark hallway. Chuckie gulped and hurried to catch up with the others, passing glowing pictures of witches and goblins along the way.

Grandpa Lou whispered to Lulu, "You know, Lu, hula night at the retirement village was much scarier than this."

But just then a goblin popped out from behind a door. "Booga, booga, booga!" it shouted.

Startled, Lou stepped back. Chuckie hid behind Dil's stroller. Tommy, Phil, and Lil laughed and clapped their hands. They loved surprises.

The goblin pretended to be scared of the babies. "Oh, no!" he said. "A hairy werewolf! And his friend, the vampire! And a witch! And two bats . . . that look alike! Oooh, scary!"

"You bet they're scary!" Grandpa Lou said. "Go get him, kids! Show him who's boss!"

Making scary noises and faces, the babies happily chased after the goblin. Dil tried to squirm out of his stroller to go too. "Not you, little spider," said Lulu. "Maybe next year."

Lulu looked up and saw the babies

were gone. "Where'd they go, Lou?"

"This way," said Lou confidently, and he headed down the wrong hallway. Lulu followed, pushing Dil in his stroller.

The babies entered a room full of curved mirrors. Angelica looked at her distorted reflection. "Beautiful as always," she said, smoothing her hair. "But nothin' is scary. This is the boringest haunted house I ever saw!"

"BLEAH! I vant to suck your blood!" Tommy popped up right in front of Angelica with his cape spread wide. Angelica jumped up and yelped.

"Ha, ha!" said Tommy. "I a-scared you, Angelica!"

"No, you didn't!" yelled Angelica. Just then, Kimi sneaked up behind her and cackled in her ear. Startled, Angelica jumped up and then stumbled backward into Phil and Lil, who started screeching like bats.

"Stop it, you guys!" said Chuckie. "You're being mean!"

Tommy looked at his friend. "We're not mean, Chuckie," he said. "We're just a-scary, like monsters is opposed to be."

"Yeah, Chuckie," said Lil. "Why do you think they call it 'Hallo*mean*'?"

Chuckie still didn't think it was right. "But, Tommy . . ."

"Oh, save it, Finster," said Angelica, embarrassed that Chuckie was sticking up for her. "Phil and Lil's diapies are scarier than this place. I'm gonna go find a *real* haunted house that doesn't let in dumb babies!"

As she left, Angelica said to herself slyly, "And can I help it if I axeldently go near Trick-or-Treat Street and a ghost axeldently gives me some candy?"

Chuckie was about to beg Angelica to stay with them when he saw another little girl dressed like a princess. Maybe

40

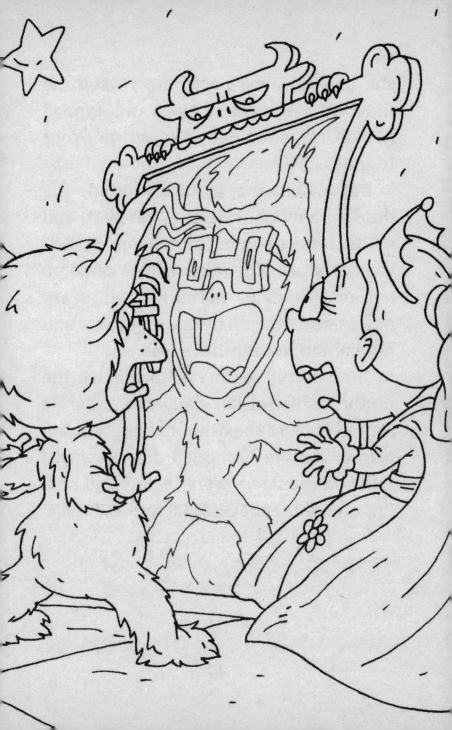

she can turn me back into myself, he thought. He walked over and tapped her on the shoulder. "Excuse me, Your Highness. . . ."

But when she turned around, the little girl saw Chuckie-the-Werewuff and all his reflections in the mirrors. "AHH!" she screamed. The other babies came up behind Chuckie, making their scary noises and faces. The little girl ran and hid behind her mother's legs.

"I'm sorry!" called Chuckie as the mother whisked her daughter away. He turned back to the other babies. "I didn't wanna a-scare her, but I did anyway! I told you monsters were mean! And now I'm one of them FOREVER and EVER!"

CHAPTER 7

Chuckie ran out of the kiddie haunted house, whipping past the wart-faced toads, black cats, and cackling witches. Once he got outside, he kept running until he reached a bunch of creepy-looking fake trees.

He stood at the entrance to the Enchanted Forest. On a high branch, he saw an owl with glowing yellow eyes. "Too scary," he said to himself, and started to turn away. Then he stopped.

"If I'm going to be a werewuff forever," Chuckie said to himself, "I guess I'd better get used to living in the woods. At least in there I won't a-scare everybody."

He was working up his courage to go

into the Enchanted Forest when Tommy, Phil, Lil, and Kimi ran up behind him.

"Chuckie, wait!" called Tommy. "What are you doing?"

"Well, since I'm a werewuff, I gots to hide out in the woods with the rest of the scary creeptures," said Chuckie. "'Cept I'm too a-scared to go in there."

Tommy put his arm around Chuckie. "Chuckie, we decided we don't wanna be monsters anymore neither."

"Really?" Chuckie asked.

They all nodded. "You were right, Chuckie," said Kimi. "Scaring people is mean."

"Even if it is kinda fun," said Phil.

Lil glared at her brother.

Chuckie smiled. "Thanks, you guys. You're the bestest friends ever."

Tommy waved for the others to follow him. "Come on! We gots to get lots and lotsa candy and give it to Angelica so she'll change us back to babies!"

"But where are we going to get lotsa candy?" asked Kimi.

"On Tricka-Treat Street!" yelled Tommy.

A long row of colorful doors lined Trick-or-Treat Street. A park employee in a Reptar costume was handing out orange bags at the entrance.

"Wow," said Phil, "it's Reptar!"

They each got a bag and then watched what the other kids did. It looked simple—walk up to a door, knock, hold open the bag . . . and get candy!

"Okay, guys," said Tommy. "Let's do it." He toddled up to the first door and knocked. The door creaked open. Chuckie hid behind Tommy.

"Oh, no!" said the ghost who opened the door. "Scary monsters! Can you say 'Trick-or-treat?'"

"No!" cried Chuckie.

"No?" said the ghost. "Well, since you're so scary, you get candy anyway." He dropped candy into everyone's bag except Chuckie's, since he was still hiding behind Tommy. Finally Chuckie stepped forward and opened his bag, trembling.

"An extra-scary werewolf should get extra candy," said the ghost, dumping so much candy in Chuckie's bag that it almost spilled out. Chuckie grinned.

"Look!" said Kimi. "There's Angelica!"

She pointed toward the big haunted house for adults. Angelica was outside the entrance munching on a licorice whip.

"Another boring haunted house," Angelica muttered to herself. "Big deal. But maybe they give you candy at the end." She ducked inside, right behind a grown-up.

"There she goes!" said Tommy. "Come on!"

"But, Tommy," said Chuckie, "that's a growed-up scary house. I don't think babies are allowed in there!"

"Babies aren't allowed," said Tommy. "But monsters like us are! Angelica hasn't changed us back yet, remember?" He hurried toward the large house. It was painted black, and the shutters were closed tightly over the windows. There were mean-looking gargoyles perched over the front door.

"I don't think this is such a good idea," said Chuckie, following the others into the house.

CHAPTER 8

Inside, they stood in a dark hallway lined with pictures of headless horsemen and evil knights. A long, gloomy corridor stretched in front of them. Ghosts howled, witches cackled, and goblins moaned. The babies huddled together, slowly moving down the hallway.

They stopped at the foot of a creaky, swaying stairway. Tommy led the way as the babies crawled up, one step at a time. Chuckie closed his eyes and held on to the railing. Finally they reached the top and saw an open door. Piano music was playing inside.

"Ya hear that? Let's go! Maybe

Angelica's in there," said Tommy.

"Yeah, or maybe it's something really s-s-scary," said Chuckie, his teeth chattering.

"Well, sometimes Angelica's scary," said Phil.

They crept into the room. There was a piano next to the window, but no one was playing it—except two hands floating in the air!

"No Angelica here, c'mon, let's go," said Chuckie all in one breath.

"Through here!" Tommy said, leading the way through a door past the piano.

Chuckie was so eager to get out of the room with the floating hands that he ran past Tommy—and right into a roomful of mummies! Their eyes glowed red in the dark. Their arms were raised up as though they were going to grab Chuckie!

"Who dares to invade our tomb?" one of them rasped. "AHH!" Chuckie screamed, and ran out.

In another room, Angelica was having her own troubles. She was trying to find her way out of the haunted house, which had turned out to be a lot scarier than she thought it would be. She opened one door after another. Then she opened a small closet, and a skeleton popped out! "Somebody get me outta this crazy place!" she screamed.

Eventually the other babies caught up with Chuckie, and they found their way out of the house. They exited through a door into the backyard, where there was a cemetery. And the only way out was to walk right past the graves!

They spotted Angelica crouched near the back door.

"Angelica!" Tommy said. "We got your candy!" They all held up their filled orange bags.

Angelica ignored the candy. "I don't care about your stupid candy!" she cried. "Just get me out of here!"

Chuckie couldn't believe his ears! After everything they'd gone through, Angelica didn't want the candy after all. "Not so fast, Angelica," he said. "First you gotta turn us back into babies!"

"First you gotta get me outta here," Angelica said with a scowl. "Lead the way!"

All of a sudden Chuckie got really mad. "NO!" he shouted. "I'm sicka being a-scared and sicka being a mean werewuff! So do what a princess does, and make me Chuckie again!"

The other babies stared at Chuckie in awe. They couldn't believe he was standing up to Angelica!

"All right!" she said. "I'll do it!" She stood up, waved her arms around the babies, and chanted, *"Finster-dee, Finster-dah, make them dumb babies again, blah blah blah!"*

The babies felt different—not like scary monsters, but like themselves.

They looked around at the creepy cemetery. "Um . . . now that we're not scary monsters, whadda we do?" asked Phil.

"I 'member what it's like to be a werewuff. I'll get us out of here," Chuckie said. "C'mon, follow me!"

The babies joined hands, and Chuckie led them through the rows of pretend graves. When a zombie popped up, Chuckie growled like a werewolf. When hands reached up out of the ground, Chuckie leaped over them on all fours. But when they finally made it through the cemetery maze they were at a dead end.

"We're trapped, Finster, trapped!" Angelica wailed. "You said you'd get me outta here!"

Chuckie stepped back. Suddenly he was teetering on the edge of a gaping hole! "YAAAAH!" he yelled, grabbing Tommy's hand as he fell backward. Angelica and the babies held hands and tumbled down the hole—one after the other.

"FINSTERRRRRR!" screamed Angelica.

CHAPTER 9

"WHEEEEE!" yelled Phil, Lil, Kimi, and Angelica as they slid down a long, twisting tunnel with flashing lights. Chuckie and Angelica were in front of them, screaming. All of a sudden—*PLOP!*—they each zipped out of the slide and landed on a big bouncy mat. It was the exit from the haunted house!

The babies gathered around Chuckie.

"Wow, Chuckie!" said Tommy. "You were really brave!"

"You weren't scared of the zombies!" said Kimi.

"You weren't scared of the ghosts!" said Lil.

"Yeah, and most of all, you weren't

even scared of Angelica!" said Phil.

Angelica wrinkled her nose. "You babies are even dumber than I thought!" she scoffed. "You were never really monsters. I tricked you!"

"That's great, Angelica!" said Tommy.

"Huh? What d'ya—," she started to say.

"Then we don't have to give you our candy!" Tommy cried.

"Oh, yes you do!" said Angelica. "I took the curse off hair and square!" She grabbed a handful of Chuckie's candy and stuffed it into her mouth. She cringed. "Blech! Yucky coconut!"

Grandpa Lou and Lulu spotted the babies across the way. They ran up, pushing Dil who was asleep in his stroller. "There you are!" said Lulu. "Thank goodness!"

Angelica rooted around in Chuckie's bag until she found a sour gumdrop. She popped it in her mouth just as the other grown-ups arrived.

"Angelica!" said Charlotte. "What do you think you're doing?"

"Mmm . . . ," mumbled Angelica, her mouth gummy with candy. "Just helping the babies unwrap their Hallomean candy." Drew and Charlotte looked at each other knowingly. "Someone needs a time-out," said Drew. "And her name is princess—er—Angelica."

"Look, Pop," said Stu proudly. "I won a ribbon for apple-bobbing!" He held up a ribbon that said EIGHTH PLACE.

"Very impressive," said Grandpa Lou. "I didn't know they gave ribbons to the losers. Why, in my day, I once bobbed for *five* apples at once, and I didn't even have any teeth! . . ."

While Grandpa Lou told his story, the babies huddled together.

"I'm confused," Chuckie said to Tommy.

"I didn't turn into a werewuff after all?"

"I guess not, Chuckeroo," said Tommy, happily digging through his bag of candy.

"But if Chuckie wasn't a werewuff," asked Lil, "how did he get so brave all of the sudden?"

"Yeah," said Phil. "Good question, Lillian."

"Thank you, Philip," said Lil.

"Maybe you acted braver," Kimi said to Chuckie, "'cause the werewuff costume made you *feel* braver."

"Or just itchier," said Chuckie.

"Hey, I gots an idea," said Tommy. "Why don't you just pretend you're dressed up like a werewuff whenever you're a-scared, and then you'll be brave all the time?"

"Yeah," said Chuckie, standing up a little straighter, "I'll be brave all the time."

"BOO!" somebody shouted.

"AHH!" screamed Chuckie, jumping up in the air.

Behind him, the little girl dressed like a princess from the kiddie haunted house giggled. "Gotcha!" she said, and ran away.

"I guess I really *am* Chuckie again," said Chuckie.

The others nodded, chewing their candy. Then Tommy spoke up.

"Since we won't turn into what we dress up as, next year I'm going to be a mummy!"

"I'm going to be a dinosaur, like Reptar!" said Phil.

"Me too!" said Lil.

"I'll be a skelly-ton!" said Kimi. They all looked at Chuckie.

"And I'll be a . . . a . . . a butterfly," said Chuckie. "Just to be safe."